The Mystery
in Dracula's Castle

by Vic Crume

Illustrated with Photos

**Based on the Walt Disney Productions' television movie
The Mystery in Dracula's Castle written by Sue Milburn.**

SCHOLASTIC BOOK SERVICES
NEW YORK · TORONTO · LONDON · AUCKLAND · SYDNEY · TOKYO

ISBN: 0-590-06859-8

Copyright © 1973 by Walt Disney Productions. All rights reserved.
Published by Scholastic Book Services, a division of Scholastic
Magazines, Inc., by arrangement with Walt Disney Productions.

15 14   9/7 01/8

Printed in the U. S.A.

01

CAST OF CHARACTERS

KEITH RAYNOR.........Clu Gulager

MARSHA BOOTH.....Mariette Hartley

ALFIE...............Johnny Whitaker

NOAH BAXTER.........Mills Watson

BILL WASDAHL.........John Fiedler

SHERIFF.............James Callahan

LEONARD..............Scott Kolden

MORGAN..........Gerald Michenaud

JEAN WYNDHAM.....Maggie Wellman

PATROLMAN.............Link Wyler

DETECTIVE..........Pete Renoudet

GRAVE ROBBER........Ben Wrigley

The Mystery
in Dracula's Castle

CHAPTER 1

DRACULA! On the shadowy screen, he glared up from his coffin, pale and horrible in the light of the grave robber's lantern!

Every pair of eyes in the dark movie house stared frozenly as Dracula's terrible bony hand reached up along the coffin edge. And when the bony fingers of the foul fiend of Transylvania curved into claws, shrieks, gasps, and moans swept the audience.

Twelve-year-old Alfie Booth, aspiring movie producer, and Morgan Harris, his best friend, weren't missing one bloodcurdling moment. Their eyes scarcely blinked. But suddenly Morgan sensed a diving motion at his side. He glanced quickly toward Alfie's young brother, Leonard. Sure enough, Leonard

had scrunched down in the seat, his fingers clamped across his eyes. Then the fingers, like Venetian blinds, widened into slits and Morgan knew that Leonard was peeking fearfully between them.

He nudged Alfie and nodded his head in Leonard's direction. Both boys chuckled, then looked quickly back at the screen where Dracula was now swirling off in a mist, his black cloak spread like batwings.

To young Leonard Booth, who had been dragged unwillingly to this Sunday matinee by his older brother, it seemed forever before a wild burst of music ended the movie and Dracula faded from view. The lights came up, and the boys straggled out into the lobby. As soon as Leonard reached the door, he hurried ahead of Alfie and Morgan, out into the wonderful light of day — the wonderful California sunshine that would have tortured Count Dracula but that ten-year-old Leonard had never loved so much as now.

Behind him, Alfie fell into step beside Morgan.

"That movie wasn't even scary," he said thoughtfully, speaking as an experienced movie producer. "I bet my film will be a lot better."

"I bet it will," Morgan agreed. "That Dracula wasn't nearly mean enough. And there should have been more blood."

Alfie frowned. "Yeah. He should have had bigger fangs. In *my* Dracula film there's going to be plenty of blood — just like in the Super-8 Frankenstein movie we made last winter. Remember?"

Morgan nodded. He angled his arms up and forward, then lurched along the sidewalk like Frankenstein. "That film was good and gory, Alfie," he said. "You're really a great director — and I was a pretty good monster too."

Leonard swung around. "I didn't like it," he said firmly.

9

"You didn't like it!" Alfie exclaimed. "What do you mean you didn't like it? What was wrong with it? You were *in* it, and you made a great Igor."

"It was awful. I'm never going to be in one of your dumb movies ever again!" Leonard burst out.

"Nobody's asking you," Alfie returned. "Any time I ask *you* to be in one of my movies again..."

"Listen!" Leonard's hand shot up. "Listen!" He started running like a bloodhound following a trail. Alfie could call himself a producer, but Leonard was a dedicated detective, and in the distance a burglar alarm was blaring.

"Who are you going to get to play Dracula in your new movie?" Morgan asked, not bothering to comment on the sounding alarm.

Alfie tugged at his ear. He sighed. "I don't know, Morg. You'd be great for the part — even better than you were in Frankenstein."

Morgan nodded in agreement. "Yeah, that's right. I'd be great. But you're going away to the beach for the summer. So that ends that. You can't have it both ways, Alfie."

"Can't have it both ways!" Alfie exclaimed. "I suppose if I was staying here, you wouldn't be going to camp? Who's leaving who, anyhow?"

Morgan sighed, "Well — what can you expect when you've got parents? Sure I'll be going to camp. But nothing would be happening around this town anyway with you gone."

10

"Hey!" Alfie exclaimed suddenly. "Flack's jewelry store! That's the big one with all the real expensive stuff. It's their burglar alarm ringing! Come on, Morg. This could be interesting."

The boys broke into a fast trot and caught up with Leonard, who was already standing in front of the jewelry store.

"Here come the police cars." Morgan said. "Let's get up on that balcony over there. We'll get a great view."

They scrambled up the stairs of the house next to the jewelry store, just as two police cars, sirens sounding, came whizzing up to the curb. Uniformed policemen and one plainclothes detective leaped out of the cars.

"What are you kids doing up there?" the detective called out. "Get down!" As the boys started down the stairs, he strode off to the shop door. "Somebody get in there and shut off that noise," he said grumpily. "Now get back, everybody. Move along."

He elbowed Leonard out of the way. "Dust this door for prints," he ordered. Striding past Alfie and Morgan, he went back to the patrol car and picked up the radio mike. "I've got a 459 here," he said. "Code 4." He put down the mike. "Any prints?" he called over to the officers.

"No prints, sir. But I think I've got something else — fibers," one of the men answered.

Leonard, standing off at one side, watched carefully. He loved detectives as much as he hated monsters. The detective flipped out a magnifying glass. He examined the rough edges of the broken glass around the lock. Then taking a pair of tweezers, he picked off some fibers and placed them in a plastic envelope.

From the other side of the door, the policeman who had gone into the shop to turn off the alarm called out: "The safe's been blown, sir."

Just then a long dark car swept up behind the parked police cars. A dignified white-haired man stepped out onto the sidewalk. "I'm Flack," he said. "This is my store. What's happened?"

The detective turned. "Mr. Flack? Well, your safe has been blown, sir."

Mr. Flack's eyes widened. He made no reply but pushed past the boys and the police and hurried into his shop. In seconds he was back, holding an empty velvet-lined tray. "It's gone! Gone!" he cried.

"What's gone, sir?"

"The Daumier jewels!" Mr. Flack gasped.

"What are the Dawm-yay jewels?" the detective asked.

Mr. Flack groaned. "Only one of the most beautiful choker necklaces in the world!" he exclaimed. "Pigeon's-blood rubies set in gold!"

"Let's go into the shop, Mr. Flack," the detective said, taking the jeweler by the arm. "Don't worry — we'll find out who did it."

"Find out who did it!" Mr. Flack cried. "Find my necklace! That's what I want!"

"The door closed behind them and Leonard moved over to the window to peer after them.

"Come on, Leonard," Alfie said. "We've got to get on home."

"Yeah. Come on," Morgan added. "They're never going to find the person who did it."

Leonard didn't budge. He watched the detective inside examining the big safe through his magnifying glass. "If I were a detective, I'd find out who did it," he said.

Alfie chuckled. "You a detective!"

Leonard turned around. "Yeah — me. Why not? I've got a magnifying glass."

Alfie held his sides laughing. "You've got to have more than that to be a detective."

Morgan grinned. "You have to have *courage*, Leonard. You have to have nerve."

"And that lets you out," Alfie said. "You'd better stick to *pretending*."

But the next day Alfie realized that his young brother was taking the detective business seriously. Instead of helping to pack the car for the trip to the beach house, Leonard was examining everything in sight through a big, round magnifying glass. Alfie looked on silently as Leonard bent over the chrome door-handle of their mother's car.

13

"Instead of searching for clues for some unknown crime, Leonard, why don't you do something useful — like searching for a place to put these?" Alfie held out a hammer and a two-foot long stake.

Just then, Marsha Booth, the boys' pretty mother, came out of the house carrying a battered old typewriter. "Alfie!" she exclaimed. "Are those things absolutely necessary? We're already loaded down."

"Yep, they're necessary," Alfie replied. "They're props for my new movie. I've decided to film *Dracula* this summer."

His mother frowned. "Does it have to be so realistic?" she asked. "Oh, well — okay. Throw them in the back seat." She walked around to the open car trunk and reached across the two bicycles that were tied above the rear bumper. "There! *Barely* enough room for my typewriter — and goodness knows I've got to get my book finished this summer. That's one thing that's absolutely necessary."

She slammed the trunk top shut. "Well that's it, boys. Let's go!"

Leonard scrambled into the driver's seat and slid over to the middle. His mother followed. Alfie hopped in on the other side, slammed the door, then shouted, "Hey! Wait! Here comes Morgan. I bet he's here to say good-bye."

"Well then, say good-bye," Leonard said shortly. He looked away from Morgan.

14

Morgan walked up to Alfie's side of the car. "Hi, Mrs. Booth. Hi, Alfie. I guess I'll see you in September." Morgan looked sadly at Alfie.

"Sure you will," Alfie answered. "In September. Say, Morgan, have a great summer at camp."

"Yes, Morgan. Have a fine summer." Mrs. Booth smiled. "You caught us just in time. We're just about to go."

Morgan sighed and stepped back from the car. Leonard lifted his magnifying glass and peered scornfully at him.

"Good-bye," Morgan said dismally.

Mrs. Booth pulled away from the curb. Alfie and Morgan kept on waving to each other.

"I'll sure miss Morgan," Alfie sighed.

"Imagine missing a guy like that," Leonard thought disgustedly. "How can Alfie stand him? Anybody would be better to have around than old Dracula Morgan."

But that was before Leonard Booth arrived at the old cottage at the beach. Before the summer was over, "Dracula Morgan" would begin to look like a dear old friend to Leonard Booth.

CHAPTER 2

Marsha Booth stopped the car in front of the family's weatherworn beach cottage.

She sighed happily. "The old town hasn't changed a bit since last summer, and neither has the cottage."

"It sure hasn't," Alfie replied in a rather gloomy voice. "Just about what I expected."

His mother breathed deeply as she stepped from the car. "Mmm! This air is so wonderful — and everything's so quiet!"

"Yeah — quiet," Leonard said dismally, following her up the walk.

Mrs. Booth looked down at the boys. "There will be plenty for all of us to do, if that's what you're thinking about. With the deadline coming up on my book,

I won't be able to spend much time with you. But,
Alfie, you're going to be busy making your film. And
you'll be helping Alfie, won't you, Leonard?"

Leonard shook his head. "No thanks. I want to be a
detective, not an actor. And there's nothing to detect
in this dead place."

Marsha Booth smiled. "Sherlock Holmes found
some of his most exciting cases on the English moors

— and I can't think of a deader place than the English moors."

Later, as Leonard bumped the last suitcase up the cottage steps, he was thinking of lonely English moors and Sherlock Holmes. "It still doesn't look too hopeful around here," he thought. "Sherlock Holmes!" He sighed. "Hmmm!"

By the time the Booth family had unpacked, settled, and finished a picnic supper on the verandah, stars were already shining above the Pacific.

Mrs. Booth yawned. "This sea air is making me sleepy," she said. "Anybody else feel like turning in?"

"Okay with me, Mom." Alfie yawned. "I want to get an early start tomorrow on the filming of my *Dracula* movie."

Leonard said nothing, but he led the way into the house.

"You can have the bed nearest the window, Leonard," Alfie said as they went into their room. "I need the wall space over this bed for my Dracula poster."

"Okay," Leonard said absentmindedly. He was examining the window screen through his magnifying glass. "Hey, Alfie! Look at this. Someone tried to get in through the window. The screen's ripped."

Alfie was trying to juggle his poster, a hammer, and a tack as he stood on his bed. He glanced toward the window screen. "You mean somebody's been trying to get *out*. That screen's pushed out, not in. I hate to say it, Leonard, but you make a lousy detective."

"Well, I'm just learning," Leonard replied calmly, putting down the magnifying glass and starting to make his bed. "Even Sherlock Holmes had to begin somewhere I guess."

A few minutes later, Alfie jumped down from his bed and stepped back to admire Dracula's fiendish face on the wall. Then he walked over to one of the two small desks in the room.

"While you're learning how Sherlock did it, I'm going to get out my Super-8 editing equipment. If I'm going to make my Dracula film, I've got to get organized."

He looked back at the poster, frowned, and sighed. "I'm never going to find anybody in this town to play Dracula."

Leonard didn't answer. He had finished making his bed and was bent over the magnifying glass again, pulling a few short strands of dark hair off the screen.

"You know, Leonard," Alfie continued, still looking at the poster, "I might just have to make you an actor again."

Leonard carefully placed the hairs on the night table by his bed. He didn't answer.

"Hey, Leonard." Alfie walked over to his brother's bed. "I said maybe I'd have to make you an actor again."

Leonard looked up. "Me? I'm not a Dracula — if that's what you're thinking. I'm not the type."

Alfie squinted at his brother. "With the right makeup it might just possibly work."

"I'm Sherlock Holmes," Leonard said firmly.

Alfie hooted. "Sherlock Holmes? *You*!"

"Why not?"

"There are a couple of reasons at least," Alfie replied. "First of all, you don't have a Watson. Everybody knows Sherlock Holmes depended a lot on his assistant. And second — whoever heard of a detective who went around detecting by peeking between his fingers?"

"I don't plan to peek," Leonard answered coolly.

"Aw, come on, Leonard. Dracula is a great character. Anybody with *guts* would jump at the chance to play Dracula."

"Not me," Leonard replied.

"Hey! What's that?" Alfie pointed to a nestlike heap of bottle caps, silver-foil gum wrappers, and one silver circle-shaped pin, in a corner of the bedroom.

Leonard picked up his magnifying glass. "Hey! It might be a clue!"

"Clue! A clue to what? Honestly, Leonard, you don't need a magnifying glass to see that. It's only a heap of junk." Alfie reached out to put the odds and ends into a nearby wastepaper basket.

"Wait, Alfie!" Leonard exclaimed. "Maybe it's a rat's nest." Leonard reached over to the night table and held up the hairs. "See. I've already found these."

"So what?" Alfie asked disgustedly. "What's so mysterious about a rat's nest?"

"It would explain the busted screen," Leonard said proudly. "A rat lives here. I've solved my first case."

Alfie groaned and rolled his eyes toward Dracula's poster. "Rats!"

Then suddenly he straightened up. "Rats! Say, that reminds me. Dracula has power over rats. All he has to do is say, 'Come here rats!' and over they come. In fact, they protect his coffin during the day."

Leonard groaned. "That guy again! Can't you get your brain on something else for a change?"

Alfie backed away and framed his hands around his eyes as though he was looking through a viewfinder. He gazed at Leonard. "You know, it would make a great scene. I'll have a big close-up of a man-eating rat — two rodent teeth dripping blood. Then I'll pull back and — " He broke off as Leonard hurriedly turned away and began examining the screen again. "Oh, go to bed! You just don't have any imagination, Leonard. Anyway, we're going to start shooting tomorrow."

Leonard didn't look as though he'd heard a word. He jumped into bed and watched as Alfie quickly made his own bed, "Hey, Alfie — leave the light on?"

Alfie promptly flipped it off. "Don't be a scaredy-cat," he said disgustedly.

Leonard didn't say a word, but his glance went to the broken window screen. Suddenly he ducked down and pulled the covers up over his eyes.

There was absolute quiet in the moonlit room.

The boys had been asleep for an hour when wild shrieks brought Alfie upright in bed, and Mrs. Booth hurrying to the boys' room.

She flicked on the light. There was Leonard hopping up and down and screeching at the top of his lungs.

"What's the *matter*?" she cried, rushing to him.

"Help! The rat, Mom! It's on my bed!"

"*Rat!*" His mother looked in horror at the rumpled bed.

Alfie blinked in the light. "Is *that* all!" he exclaimed. "I thought something must be really wrong. You just think you saw a rat."

"I did. I did!" Leonard cried. "I heard it scratching and gnawing. *It's on the bed now*! Look!" He pointed toward the foot of his bed.

Even Alfie had to admit that there was a large bump under the covers. He looked at it admiringly. "Say, that's the biggest rat I ever saw."

Marsha Booth fearfully eyed the bumped-up covers. As she looked the bump moved beneath the blankets. "Stand back, boys," she ordered, then walked grimly toward the bed. With a quick flick she pulled the covers away.

"It's a dog!" the Booth boys cried out in one voice.

Mrs. Booth laughed in relief. "And a nice one. With fleas too, I suppose. There! He's wagging his tail at us. Come on, doggie. We're not going to hurt you!" She turned to the boys. "I wonder how on earth he got in here?"

The dog, a raggedy, bright-eyed little mutt, looked from one member of the family to another, yawned, and curled up again.

"Looks like he's staying too," Mrs. Booth said. "Squatters' rights, I guess you'd call it."

"Can we really keep him?" Leonard asked excitedly.

"As long as he wants to keep us," his mother answered.

Leonard leaned over and patted the newcomer. "I think I'll call you Watson," he said.

"Watson!" Alfie exclaimed. "Some people can't think about anybody but Sherlock Holmes."

"And some people can't think about anybody but Dracula," Leonard said calmly.

Mrs. Booth laughed. "And I know one person who can't think about anybody but Sleeping Beauty — and that's me." She flicked off the light. "Goodnight, boys. You too, Watson."

The door closed, and once again the room was flooded with moonlight.

Alfie punched at his pillow. "Don't forget, Leonard — we have to be on location early. Get some sleep."

Leonard wriggled his toes until they pressed against Watson, who had already settled down for the night. "Where's 'location,' Alfie?"

Alfie gave his pillow another punch. "I don't know yet," he said crossly. "That's why we have to get up early. We've got to *find* one."

CHAPTER 3

Late afternoon shadows were growing long and steep before Alfie found the ideal location to begin filming his horror movie.

He looked along the length of the alleyway that ran past the sheriff's office and the town jail. "Filming is running far behind schedule," he said sternly. "But I think this alley might work out as an outdoor set. Leonard, put on your cape and go over there," Alfie pointed out a distance up the alley, "then turn around and run toward me *fast*. Make your cape fly out. I want you to look batlike."

Leonard started off, Watson at his heels. When Leonard was in position, Alfie lifted the camera.

"Now, run," he called. "Wait! Wait, Leonard. Get that dog out of there. Who ever heard of Dracula with a dog?"

Before five more minutes had passed, Alfie was desperate. "Leonard, that dog's got to go. This is the third take he's ruined."

Leonard skidded to a stop and looked back over the shoulder of his long black Dracula cape. "Go back, Watson!" he managed to say in spite of the fact that the sharp pearly fangs he was wearing made speech a little difficult.

Just then the sheriff of the small beach town, Sheriff Wyndham, stepped out of the back door of his office. "Is that stray bothering you?" he asked.

"Yes," Alfie said shortly.

"No," Leonard exclaimed. "He's a good dog."

The sheriff grinned. "Good for nothing, you mean. That's the thievingest mutt in the county. I'm going to have to do something about him sometime. He thinks he owns the place."

"He sure does," Alfie said grumpily.

"Trouble — that's the name for him. Wherever that dog goes — and the dog goes everywhere — there goes Trouble."

Leonard took off the pearly fangs and dropped them in his pocket. He bent down and put his arms around Watson. "His name *isn't* Trouble. It's *Watson.*"

"You can call him anything you like, son. He's still Trouble to me."

As the sheriff turned he saw that Bill Wasdahl, the man who owned the small jewelry store across the street, was locking up for the day. "Say, now, I have to catch Bill before he leaves. I meant to see him earlier." He looked at Watson. "Seriously kids, keep an eye on that dog. He'll steal you blind. And you'd better find another location for your filming. I don't want you playing around the jail."

"I thought Mr. Wilson was the sheriff," Alfie said, glancing at the star on the sheriff's jacket.

"Wilson retired. I've taken his place. The name is Wyndham. Now run along, kids." He looked at Alfie. "Anyone with your imagination can find another location, I'll bet."

Alfie sighed. "This is just about the best alley in town. But okay. I guess we can find another. Come on, Leonard. Put your fangs back on. I want to get this outdoor shot before the light goes."

"Bill, I know you were just leaving, but this won't take a minute," Sheriff Wyndham called out to the jeweler as he hurried up to the shop door. "I want to show you something."

"Sure. Come on in the shop," Bill Wasdahl replied.

As the sheriff stepped into the little shop he glanced around at the small display cases. "I see you've put in a new line of watches, Bill. Real nice."

Bill Wasdahl nodded. "Thanks. What was it you wanted to show me?" He glanced at his wristwatch. "I'm in kind of a hurry."

Sheriff Wyndham fumbled through his pockets. "Here it is — a photo." He handed it to the jeweler. "Have you seen this? It's a necklace — seven rubies set in gold."

The jeweler looked at the picture. "No. Should I have?"

The sheriff shook his head. "Beats me why they send me this stuff. This town would be the last place

I'd expect to find a stolen necklace. Especially one worth a hundred thousand dollars."

Bill Wasdahl whistled and took another look at the photograph. "That's a lot of money." He handed back the picture.

"No, you keep it. You'd be the most likely person around here to see this Daumier necklace. Jewel thieves don't trust us sheriffs." The sheriff laughed and slapped Bill Wasdahl's shoulder. "Well, so long, Bill. See you tomorrow." He turned toward the front door. "*Now* what!" he exclaimed.

Out on the street Watson had his muzzle pressed against the plate glass window, and Leonard Booth was trying his best to tug him away.

The late afternoon sunlight glinted on the display in the jeweler's window, and Watson was enchanted by the sight. He had zoomed past Dracula Booth and rushed to the shining window, while Leonard rushed after him.

Now Alfie, almost bouncing up and down in anger, shouted after him: "Leonard! You're not supposed to leave until I say 'cut' or 'take five' or something!"

Leonard tugged at Watson. "I couldn't help it, Alfie. Come help me. What do you think is wrong with him?"

"You've got a thief on your hands, all right," Alfie replied as he walked up to the window. "I sure don't know what he sees in this junk." And then his gaze lighted upon a gold ring with a black center.

"Hey, Leonard. Look at that! Dracula's ring!"

Leonard stared at the display. "I don't see anything special."

"Dracula always has a ring," Alfie said excitedly. "And that one's perfect."

Just then Bill Wasdahl and the sheriff came to the door. "Get that mutt away from my store," the jeweler said.

"He wasn't doing anything," Leonard said, rubbing Watson's ear.

The jeweler stepped out into the street, took out a handkerchief, and began polishing Watson's nose prints off the window. "He's ruining my property," he said.

"He is not!" Leonard said angrily. "He was just *looking*."

"Well, he can look some other place," Bill Wasdahl said.

Alfie frowned. "We're here to do business," he said coldly, and patted Watson's other ear.

"Oh?"

"How much is that ring there? The gold one with the black-eyed center."

"Thirty dollars," the jeweler said curtly.

Alfie whistled. "*Thirty*! Would you rent it?"

"No."

"How about lending it to me? I'm making a Dracula movie, and I'd give you a screen credit," Alfie said.

"No."

It was not a conversation that interested Watson. He quietly slipped away from Alfie and Leonard, and trotted into the shop. Immediately he spotted the same wristwatch display that Sheriff Wyndham had noticed. He jumped up, seized a silver watchband, and trotted out of the shop — taking a shortcut between the jeweler's legs.

"Watson!" Leonard cried. "Stop! Watson, *please* stop!"

Bill Wasdahl shouted out, "Stop him. Thief! Stop!"

It was no use. Watson was off, and running straight for the art exhibit spread out in the town square. Out of the corner of his eye he saw Leonard, cape flying, streaking after him. Behind Leonard came Alfie. And pounding after Alfie came the sheriff and the jeweler.

"Make a circle! Box him in!" Sheriff Wyndham shouted.

Watson knew there was no time to lose. He dived into the thick of things. Easels toppled and scattered left and right. Artists leaped to snatch paintings back to safety. Shrieks of dismay pierced the usual quiet of the town square. Watson had never seen so many pairs of legs in all his life — and they were all crowding closer and closer.

There was only one thing to do — and Watson did it. He circled and dodged, then at top speed, dived toward Bill Wasdahl's trousered legs. *Wham*! The jeweler staggered, lurched, and tumbled to the grass.

Luckily for Watson, Leonard's cape billowed over the jeweler's face. In the tangle that followed, Watson zoomed off across the street, and through the open door of Mr. Petrocini's fish market. Just as he was leaping over a tank of live lobsters, Leonard came panting through the doorway.

Watson took a hasty look around. The situation was bad. Mr. Petrocini and a customer were blocking the way ahead and Leonard was closing in from behind. Watson could see no way to go but up. And up he went — square into a big bin of icy, slippery fish.

"My fish!" screamed Mr. Petrocini. "My fish!" He rushed to the rescue, grabbing up a broom on the way. Watson eyed the batting straws in alarm, but he hung onto the silver watchband with all his might. Then in one giddy jump, he sailed into the air and landed in the weighing pan of the old-fashioned scales that hung down from the ceiling. And there he swung, all fifteen pounds of him, sizing up the situation. The situation wasn't improving. Mr. Petrocini came charging after him, and brought the broom smashing down on the edge of the scale. Once again, Watson gathered his shaggy self for a soaring jump. This time he sailed over everybody, shot out onto the sidewalk, and across the street — and leaped through the open door of a parked Volkswagen.

The chase was over! A hand closed down on him and a firm voice said, "Come here, dog!"

Watson knew a businesslike command when he heard one. He felt himself being lifted. There was no escape! Meekly, he allowed his silver treasure to be removed by the man who held him.

Leonard, followed by Bill Wasdahl, came running up to the car.

"Watson!" Leonard cried.

The big man looked at Leonard and dropped Watson into his outstretched arms. He looked toward Bill Wasdahl and held out the watchband. "Is this your property?"

"It certainly is! Thanks," the jeweler said. He examined the watchband. "No teethmarks — if you can believe it! The way that mutt was hanging on to it, I thought it would be all chewed up. Thanks again."

"Don't mention it," the big man answered. He stepped into his car and drove off.

The jeweler turned to Leonard. "I want you to keep that dog away from my store. Understand? If I see him sneaking around my place just *once*, I'll...I'll...."

With Watson still in his arms, Leonard backed away — and right into Alfie.

"Come on, Leonard," Alfie said, giving Bill Wasdahl a chilly stare and giving Watson a pat on the head. "Let's go home."

As the boys began to walk away, Sheriff Wyndham came puffing up.

"Now, Bill — don't get all flustered," the sheriff said. "After this those boys just might keep Trouble out of trouble."

"They'd better!" the jeweler answered darkly.

Noah Baxter, whose Volkswagen Watson had tried to hide in, sped along the narrow, sand-bordered road to the ocean. He slowed the car as he neared a steep driveway that led to an old lighthouse perched on high rocks jutting out into the sea. At the edge of the drive was a neatly painted sign: KEITH RAY-NOR — ARTIST. Noah swung the Volkswagen up the lane and honked the car's horn twice.

From the glass-enclosed lantern gallery at the top of the lighthouse, Keith Raynor heard the signal. He put down his sketch pad and hurried down the iron staircase.

When he stepped outside, Keith wasted no words in greeting Noah Baxter. "Where've you been?" he asked. "I expected you days ago. Did you get it?"

Noah grinned. "Did I ever fail you? Here." He handed over a brown-wrapped parcel.

Keith Raynor tore off the wrapping and held up a framed oil painting. "What's the idea? I didn't order this."

"I think you did," Noah answered. He gave Keith a pocketknife. "Use this," he said.

34

Keith hesitated, then began cutting the canvas away from the frame. He caught his breath. *"Beautiful!"*

There between the painted canvas and the backing of the frame was the thing Keith Raynor had been waiting for — seven pigeon's-blood rubies set into a golden necklace. The Daumier jewels!

Noah Baxter took a bulky canvas bag from the Volkswagen, then reached back for a long pine box. "Chisels, mallets, jimmy-bar, explosives," he said. "I'm going to know exactly what I'm doing on the next job. I've spotted a wall safe exactly like the one I'll have to blow on the San Francisco heist. I'll bring it back here tomorrow. Come on, help me carry this."

The two men carried Noah's supplies into a low building that had been used for storing oil when the lighthouse was still in operation. Now it served as Keith's living quarters. Keith put the canvas bag on the work table, then faced his companion. "What's the point in blowing an empty safe, Noah?"

"I thought I'd just told you," Noah answered as he opened the bag.

Keith shook his head. "Why did you get more dynamite? You already have a box of it upstairs. You've got enough supplies here to blow three safes. It's dangerous."

"Don't you worry about me," Noah said sharply. "Just you get those rubies into a new setting so we

can sell them. And remember — nothing fancy.
Don't get to thinking you're a real artist."

Keith glared back and turned away.

"Oh, one more thing, Keith," Noah called after
him. "When I get back I'll need help. Those wall
safes are heavy."

Saying no more, he slammed out the door. In seconds, he was swirling the little car down the drive and
onto the roadway.

CHAPTER 4

The next morning, Alfie was faced with a problem. His mother, who had heard about Watson's adventure the day before, declared the town off limits as a place for filming the Dracula story. That left only the beach to explore.

"First I get Watson and now I get a beach!" Alfie said disgustedly. "Perhaps I should show Dracula going surfing?"

"He'd have to do it at night," Leonard reminded him.

Alfie's eyes gleamed. "With a shark escort!" he exclaimed. "That'd be great, Leonard."

Leonard set down his juice glass. "And you could have a horde of rats waiting for him on the beach.

They could be holding up a cape — only it would really be a big beach towel. They could be holding it up in their teeth."

Alfie eyed Leonard sharply. "You're silly — did you know that?"

"Well, it was only an idea," Leonard replied serenely.

"If that's your idea of an idea..." Alfie began. Then he pushed back his chair. "Come on, Leonard. We've got to get started. Yesterday was a big nothing."

An hour later they were on the beach. Alfie, his camera poised for a good shot, paced along with Leonard. Watson followed, stopping now and then to examine interesting bubbles in the sand as the surf rolled back.

"Leonard!" Alfie, as usual, was holding his hands in front of his eyes, using them as a viewfinder.

Leonard looked up.

"Leonard! Look! That's it — Dracula's Castle!"

Leonard followed Alfie's line of vision. "That old lighthouse?" he asked in surprise.

"It's perfect," Alfie said excitedly. "Why didn't I think of it before! Come on, Leonard."

"How do we get up there?" Leonard asked, eyeing the high rocks above them.

"There must be a way somewhere. Let's look."

Alfie was right. Farther up the beach they found

some steps that led up along the rocks to the light-house; it didn't take the boys and Watson long to reach the top.

"This place has probably been deserted for years," Alfie exclaimed. "It'll be just great!"

Leonard bent over a set of tire tracks cut into the sand. He took out his magnifying glass. "Tracks," he announced. "Fresh tracks. Look."

But Alfie wasn't listening. He was sizing up the possibilities for filming the circular tower and the connecting oblong building. "That was probably used for a garage, I guess," Alfie said, pointing to the storage building. "It's the lighthouse itself I'd film — Dracula's Castle! And we wouldn't be bothering anybody here. Come on, Leonard. Let's see if we can get inside."

Leonard hung back. "Alfie, we'd better not."

Alfie groaned. "I might have known — scared again."

"I am not!"

"Then come on." Alfie marched around to the entrance of the lighthouse and turned the doorknob. The door creaked spookily and swung inward.

"Man! Hear that creak!" Alfie's voice rose with excitement. He closed and then opened the door again. "Listen to that! Wow! If I only had sound equipment!" He stepped into the building and Watson squeezed past him.

"Watson!" Leonard called out softly. "Come back."

But Watson was as interested as Alfie in exploring. Leonard hesitated, then stepped inside.

Hazy sunlight filtered through the windows, making shadow patterns on the circular staircase. Alfie almost jumped in delight. "Look at those shadows! Look at those stairs! What a shot!" He looked up into

the iron skeleton of the circular stairs. "I know just how I'd do it — Dracula climbing up, up, up. And his shadow would be like a bat, and it would loom across the walls at every step."

There was no reply from Leonard. He was paying no attention to shadows, but he was paying a lot of attention to the things spread out on the worktable. He didn't need his magnifying glass to see the mallets, chisels, and jimmy-bar, but he whipped the glass out of his pocket to examine more closely the letters printed on the box on the table: DYNAMITE.

"Hey, Alfie," he called. "Alfie."

"I'm up here," Alfie's voice called back from the next floor. "Come on up. I've just discovered somebody's laboratory!"

Leonard's heart thumped. Where there were laboratories there were usually mad scientists. And about the last thing Leonard wanted to do was to discover a mad scientist. But almost anything was better than being alone with a box of dynamite. Slowly, he went up the winding stairs to the second floor.

At the top floor of the lighthouse, in the seclusion and bright light of the glassed-in lantern gallery, Keith Raynor heard the voices of the uninvited visitors. Hastily he lifted the Daumier necklace off the drawing board and slipped it into his pocket. Then he went quickly to the open trap-door and looked down the staircase.

Alfie's voice floated up to him. "This is the place where mad scientists do their experiments. Just look at all those bottles and tubes!"

Then he heard Leonard's quavering voice: "What kind of experiments?"

"Transplants... brains, glands, hands, *every-thing*," came the reply. "You know, Frankenstein, Wasp Woman."

Why, it was only two kids and a dog. One of the kids was dressed in a funny-looking long black cape. Keith crept on down.

Watson suddenly gave a low growl.

"Alfie." Leonard grabbed his brother. "Let's get out of here."

"What are you kids doing down there?" Keith Raynor called out roughly. He came thumping the rest of the way down the stairs.

Leonard's voice trembled out. "Are you the mad scientist?"

Keith Raynor burst out laughing. He flicked a light switch and immediately the "mad scientist's laboratory" turned into an artist's workshop. Daubs of color were everywhere and sheet-draped canvas paintings were propped around the walls. "No. I'm not a mad scientist. I'm an artist — Keith Raynor. And who are you? Dracula?"

"Oh, no," Leonard answered quickly. "I'm Leonard Booth. And this is my dog, Watson."

"And I'm Alfie," said Alfie.

"I wish I could say I was glad to meet you," Keith Raynor said. "Do you want to explain why you're here, or should I call the sheriff?"

Alfie gasped. "The sheriff! What for? We haven't done anything."

"No?" replied the artist. "I'd say you've done something — it's called 'breaking and entering.'"

"We didn't break anything," Alfie said.

"The door wasn't locked. We just entered," Leonard added, truthfully.

Keith Raynor looked from one boy to the other. "Why?"

Alfie spoke up. "I'm making a film — *Dracula*. My brother's playing the lead role. And this would be a great location — it's really a weird layout."

"It looks like a torture chamber," Leonard said.

Keith Raynor smiled. "First time I've heard an artist's workshop called a torture chamber." He waved his hand toward the paints, brushes, and easels. "I paint pictures for a living."

"Then what's the dynamite for?" Leonard asked.

"*Dynamite*!" Keith Raynor and Alfie Booth exclaimed together.

"Yes, dynamite. It's on the table downstairs."

There was a long pause. Then Keith Raynor laughed. "Oh, *that*. You mean my fireworks. I had to label them 'dynamite' just in case the sheriff saw the

box. You know fireworks are unlawful in this county."

"Real fireworks?" Alfie asked. "Wow! Are you going to set them off on the Fourth of July?"

Keith Raynor looked uneasy. "Oh, no! Labor Day, maybe."

"Maybe I could work them into a movie," Alfie said eagerly.

"Maybe you could," the artist replied. "But if you want to help me with the fireworks on Labor Day you'll have to go now."

Alfie sighed. "Too bad. This really *is* Dracula's Castle."

"Sorry," Keith Raynor said. "But that's the way it has to be."

Alfie nodded sadly. "Okay. Come on, Leonard. I'll just have to change the shooting schedule again."

As the boys and Watson left the lighthouse and started down the driveway, the door behind them closed and locked. Alfie looked back. "Listen, Leonard — I want to get some shots of the castle. You go back to the steps. It'll just take us a second."

"But the man said — " Leonard began.

"Go on, Leonard," Alfie said firmly. "It'll be all right."

No sooner had Alfie spoken, than Noah Baxter swung the Volkswagen into the drive. The boys ducked out of sight, but Watson, who had just settled himself, didn't stir.

"We'd better go, Alfie," Leonard urged.

Alfie shook his head. "I've just got to get my title shot, at least. Wait, Leonard. He'll be going in. They won't notice us."

Noah Baxter stopped the car at the entrance to the storage room and honked the horn twice. Almost immediately, Keith Raynor opened the door.

Noah stepped from the car. "Give me a hand with this," the boys heard him say.

As the two men lifted a small but heavy safe from the seat of the car, Noah dropped the shiny car keys. Like a shot from a gun, Watson was after them. Silver — his favorite color!

Without thinking, Noah Baxter dropped his end of the safe, nearly crushing Keith Raynor's toes. He was off at top speed after Watson, who had already skidded to a stop and dropped the keys at Leonard's feet.

"What are you kids doing here?" he called out angrily.

"We're making a film," Alfie called back. "Mr. Raynor knows all about it."

"Making a *film!*" Noah exclaimed. He strode up to the boys, picked up the car keys, and grabbed Alfie's camera.

"Hey! that's mine," Alfie exclaimed. "Give it back."

Keith Raynor caught up with Noah. "Give him back his camera, Noah," he said quietly. "I'll take care of this."

"You'd better!" Noah scowled as he returned the camera to Alfie.

Keith Raynor looked from Leonard to Alfie. "I asked you boys in a nice way to go. Now I'll have to do something drastic. I'll have to speak to your parents."

Alfie and Leonard looked at each other, and then up at Keith Raynor.

"Our *parent*, you mean," Leonard said. "We've only got one."

Alfie said nothing. He knew that in a case like this, one parent was drastic enough.

Mrs. Booth was just opening the screeen door as Alfie, Leonard, Watson, and Keith Raynor came up the porch steps.

"Mrs. Booth?" Keith asked.

"Yes?" Marsha Booth glanced quickly at Alfie and Leonard. They were staring down at their sneakers. Even Watson had a guilty look. She looked back at the stranger.

"I'm Keith Raynor. I live in the old lighthouse on the beach."

The boys' mother hesitated. "Won't you come in?" she asked.

"Thank you," Keith replied. "But I'm afraid this isn't a social call. You see, I found your boys filming at the lighthouse — or planning to, that is. It isn't safe around there. There've been rock slides recently."

"Oh," Marsha Booth looked relieved. "Then all you have to do is to tell Alfie to keep away and he'll keep away."

Keith Raynor shook his head. "I tried that. It

48

didn't work. I wouldn't want to suggest anything
since we've just met, but maybe the boys need more
supervision — if you know what I mean."

"Yes, I'm afraid I do," the boys' mother replied.
"Thank you for your concern, Mr. Raynor. I'll make
sure they won't bother you again."

"Thank you. Good-bye, Mrs. Booth." Keith got up
and started for the door.

"Mr. Raynor!" Leonard hurried after him and tugged at Keith's sleeve. He lowered his voice. "We can still light the fireworks, can't we?"

Keith hesitated. He looked at Leonard's eager face. "Oh, I guess so... before you leave."

Leonard beamed. "Good-bye, Mr. Raynor. We'll see you Labor Day."

But when Leonard went back in the house, his smile faded. A very serious-looking parent faced her two sons.

"I know I depend on you boys a lot to take care of yourselves," she began, looking from Alfie to Leonard. "Maybe too much. But you know I can't be with you all day."

Alfie and Leonard for the second time that morning looked down at their sneakers. And Watson turned his back on everybody, as though the whole scene was too much for him.

"So," Mrs. Booth continued, "since you can't seem to take care of yourselves, I'll just have to find someone to help." She picked up the local newspaper and turned to the want ads.

Alfie made a long face.

"You needn't look that way," his mother said. "You brought this on yourself. Anyway, an older playmate will be good for you."

"Playmate! You mean baby-sitter!" Alfie said.

Marsha Booth grinned. "That's what I mean," she answered cheerfully.

50

She looked back at the newspaper. "Hmm! Here's a possibility — Jean Wyndham, sixteen, experienced dog-walker, piano teacher, surfboard sander, mother's helper, baby-sitter. Fifty cents an hour, 203 Main Street." She circled the ad.

"She sure can do a lot of things," Leonard said.

"But nothing we can use," Alfie added quickly, at the same time giving Leonard a nudge in the ribs.

"Why not?" Marsha Booth said. "A mother's helper is just what I'm looking for. Let's go, boys."

"Wyndham," Alfie muttered. "That's the sheriff's name. This Jean person probably belongs to his family. And she's probably a jailer-type."

"Maybe she's only a distant relative," Leonard said hopefully.

But hope faded when the Booths and Watson arrived at 203 Main Street. The man mowing the small front lawn was none other than the sheriff himself. Alfie looked alarmed. "Mom, are you sure you want to do this?"

"Certainly, I'm sure," his mother answered, and proceeded up the front walk.

Sheriff Wyndham looked up and cut the power on the mower.

"I'm Marsha Booth," Mrs. Booth said smiling. "We're looking for Jean Wyndham. The ad in the newspaper gave this address."

"You're at the right place, all right," the sheriff replied. He turned toward the house. "Jeanie," he

51

called. Then he turned back to Marsha Booth. "Is this for dog-walker, piano teacher, mother's helper, or surfboard sander?" He grinned.

"Mother's helper," Marsha Booth replied.

A tall deeply tanned girl with long straight hair came out of the house and down the steps.

"Mrs. Booth, here, is interested in a mother's helper, Jeanie," the sheriff said.

"Hi, Mrs. Booth." Jean Wyndham smiled.

"And here are Alfie and Leonard," the sheriff continued with the introductions. "I met them yesterday. And I guess you already know Trouble."

Leonard scowled. "Watson," he said, not quite under his breath.

Jean bent down and patted the small dog. "Hiya, Watson!"

She couldn't have done a nicer thing. Leonard's scowl disappeared.

"Jean," Mrs. Booth began, "I'm a writer and I've a deadline to meet. So I just can't spend all the time with the boys I'd like to. It would be a big help to me if you could go around with them — play with them as a friend."

Alfie rolled up his eyes in despair, but Jean Wyndham didn't seem to notice. "Sure, Mrs. Booth. That'd be great." She turned to Alfie. "Are you the film maker my dad was telling me about?"

Alfie nodded in a haughty sort of way. "Yes. I'm making a movie."

Jean smiled. "I've always wanted to be in the movies. Do you think you could work in a part for me?"

Alfie's eyebrows lifted slightly. "What acting experience have you had?" he asked coolly.

"Oh, lots! I was Desdemona in our high school play *Othello* last year, just to name one thing."

Alfie didn't want to appear too interested, so he just said, "Okay. I'll try you. But remember, I said *try*. This isn't a contract."

A plan was forming in Alfie's mind. Maybe this mother's helper was a blessing in disguise. He needed a girl to play the part of Dracula's victim, and Jean Wyndham was pretty, he had to admit. "I'll begin filming tomorrow morning," he thought to himself. "We'll film on the beach with the lighthouse and the rocks for a background."

CHAPTER 5

The next morning when Jean arrived at the beach cottage, Alfie set his plan into action. "I think you'd better wear your swimming suit," he said to Jean. "And if you have a beach robe, that'll be good. I want you to look kind of angelic — and kind of *toothsome* too."

Jean nodded. "Toothsome for Leonard's fangs, I expect. Sure Alfie."

Alfie looked pleased. "That's it. And follow what I say, Jean. You know it takes a great director to make a great actress." He looked around at Leonard. "And that goes for you too, Dracula. Follow my direction."

Leonard blinked. "Alfie, you're never going to make a great *actress* out of me."

"You know what I mean, Leonard," Alfie said sternly. "Now go get your fangs and cape while Jean gets on her swimming suit. I'd like to catch the morning sun so I can get some interesting shadows."

The place Alfie chose for filming was on the beach near the lighthouse steps. "Now I'm going to switch back and forth between you for shots. Leonard's a little short for you, Jean. But I'll zoom in on both of you for the close-ups."

He reached in his pocket and handed Jean a small gold cross. "Here. When Dracula bends over your throat, you screech and hold this up. Everybody knows Dracula is powerless when a cross comes between him and his victim." He paused. "Now, Leonard — when Jean holds it up, you step back in horror."

"Why?" asked Leonard.

"Because the power of goodness is stopping you and you can't stand it.

"Okay, now. Positions, everybody. *Action*."

In spite of Alfie's clear instructions, when Jean screamed and held up the cross, Leonard looked at it, shrugged his caped shoulders, and walked away.

"Leonard! What do you think you're doing?" Alfie exclaimed angrily.

"I'm shocked and I step back in horror — just like you said," Leonard answered.

Alfie groaned. "But you're not *showing* it! How

can you look shocked by just bumping up your shoulders?" He twitched his own shoulders up and down and Jean giggled.

Leonard whirled away. "I never wanted to play your old Dracula anyhow," he burst out.

"Aw, Leonard, you can do it. Look. Watch me." Alfie swooped up to Jean, stopped suddenly, hissed in horror, and flung himself on the sand. "See, Leonard? I'm showing I'm completely stopped by the power of goodness."

"Okay." Leonard answered quickly. "You be the one to get stopped. I'll call 'action.'"

Above them, in the storage room of the lighthouse, Noah Baxter was having harder problems even than Alfie. He had the job of hooking up a charge of explosives to the practice safe — and he was in a bad mood.

"Getting fireworks for those kids was stupid," he snapped at Keith. "For one thing, they're illegal. And for another, I don't want the kids here anytime — that goes for Labor Day too."

Keith Raynor shrugged. "You don't see them hanging around here, do you? Telling them they could come on Labor Day is why you're having privacy now. And as far as fireworks being illegal — what you're doing now isn't exactly legal, is it?"

Noah glared at him angrily. Instead of glaring

back, Keith pointed to his workroom on the top of the lighthouse. "Right now," he said, "I'm worrying more about that charge going off. I've got a lot of valuable things up there, including a certain very hot necklace."

Noah scowled. "Will you stop it? I'm the best explosives man on the West Coast. I can do this blindfolded."

Keith eyed the fuse Noah was handling. "Maybe you can, but I think I'll just take a walk — check the car, or something."

"Nothing is going to happen," Noah retorted. He struck a match. "All you have to do is cover your ears. One *pop*, and that's it." He lighted the fuse.

Down on the beach the director and the cast of *Dracula* heard a heavy *boom*. Watson dived into Leonard's cape.

"What was that!" Jean Wyndham exclaimed. She jumped up.

Leonard pointed up toward the lighthouse. "There's a lot of black smoke."

"Dracula's Castle!" Alfie exclaimed. "Something's happening to it!"

"And maybe something's happening to Mr. Raynor," Leonard quavered.

Jean didn't hesitate. She rushed toward the steps, Alfie, Leonard, and Watson at her heels.

Black smoke and dust clouds were still rolling from the storage-room windows as they reached the top step. Jean darted for the door. As she put her hand on the doorknob, the door was flung back. Keith Raynor and Noah Baxter, both smoke-blackened, staggered out.

"Are you all right?" Jean gasped.

"Okay," Keith Raynor replied, quickly blocking her view through the open door. "I — I was lighting the stove. I guess there must have been a gas leak, and gas had built up."

"Everything's under control," Noah added.

"We heard it all the way down on the beach," Alfie panted. "What a shot! If I'd only had my camera ready!"

Noah Baxter laughed unpleasantly. "We'll try to time it better for you next time." He suddenly whirled around. "Hey! That dog!"

Watson was edging past Keith Raynor's legs and heading into the building.

"I'll get him," Leonard said. He hurried forward. "Watson! Come back here!"

Noah Baxter snatched Leonard by the cape. "You just stay here, kid. *I'll* get him." He strode off, calling "Watson! Come back here, you mutt!"

Watson didn't bother to even look back. He trotted into the storage room, took one sniff, and proceeded up the staircase.

On the top floor, something glinting in the sunlight caught Watson's attention — the Daumier necklace on Keith Raynor's drawing table. For a clearer view, Watson jumped on a chair.

"You'd like that, wouldn't you, dog?" a hard voice said behind him. "Even better than the car keys." Watson felt himself being swooped up and swiftly carried down the stairs he had just climbed.

In no time, Noah was back in the doorway with Watson under his arm. He tossed the little dog to the ground. "Here's your mutt," he said. "G'bye."

"Can we help you clean up?" Jean asked politely.

"No, it's not that bad," Keith Raynor replied. He stepped back into the building.

"G'bye," Noah said again, and swung the door shut.

"*Well!*" Jean exclaimed indignantly.

They looked at each other, shrugged, and turned away. All but Watson. He was scratching at the closed door. "Come on, Watson," Leonard said, pulling him away. "We're going home."

Alfie turned toward the steps leading down to the beach. "Not that way," Jean said. "It's late. We'll take the bush path. It's shorter."

They walked along in silence until Leonard exclaimed, "Look at that!" He pointed to a large drainpipe about four feet across and half covered by rusty, bent screening. "It used to be a cave, I bet," Leonard said excitedly.

Alfie sighed. "Honestly, Leonard. How could a cave 'used to be'? If it ever was, it still is, isn't it?"

Jean laughed. "It's no cave — now or ever," she said, "just a big drainpipe. The other end comes out at Town Lake. It makes a kind of little waterfall there whenever we get a really heavy rain."

She looked down at Leonard. "You know — I've just been thinking. I hate to say it, Leonard, but I know now why my dad calls Watson 'Trouble.'"

Leonard looked hurt. "He's just curious, that's all," he said loyally. "Aren't you, Watson?" He looked around. No Watson was in sight.

"Oh no! Not again," Alfie groaned.

"I'll go back and get him," Leonard said, swirling his cape.

Jean grabbed at it. "No you don't! Don't worry, Leonard. That dog can take care of himself. He knows the way home. Come on, kids. It's late."

Watson was not a dog to give up easily — not where a bright shiny treasure was concerned. And luck was with him!

Broom in hand, Noah Baxter opened the storage-room door. As he swept a heap of sooty ashes outside and whisked them into the sand near the entrance, Watson saw his chance. When the man's back was turned, he scooted through the door and lost no time in reaching that interesting top floor.

Keith Raynor was sitting at the table working

carefully on the very thing Watson had come to view — and take home, if possible.

Keith lifted the third ruby from its setting, put it into a small box on the table, then began to chip lightly at the setting of the fourth ruby.

Watson trotted over, sat down by the chair, and thumped his tail cheerfully to signal his arrival.

Keith looked down. "How did you get in here?" he asked. Then a worried look came over his face. "Noah!" he called. "Are those kids back again?"

"No," came the answering shout.

Watson thumped his tail again and whined pleadingly.

Keith put down the necklace. "You hungry?"

Watson obliged with a sad whine and Keith pushed back his chair. "Okay. Okay. I'll get you a cookie or something."

When Keith disappeared down the stairs, Watson leaped onto the empty chair. From there it was no trouble at all to seize the glittering gold necklace. He didn't stop to admire it — there would be time for that later. He bounced down from the chair, rushed for the stairs, and nearly collided with Keith Raynor on his way back up.

"Hey!" Keith exclaimed. "Couldn't you wait?"

Watson bounced past him, the necklace swinging from side to side.

"Noah!" Keith shouted, horrified. "Stop that mutt! He's got the jewels!"

Too late! Watson was already out the door and into the knee-high grass on the land side of the lighthouse.

In seconds, Noah and Keith were in hot pursuit.

"Where'd he go?" Keith panted, searching for any movement in the grass.

"Over there!" Noah leaped ahead.

They were just in time to see Watson scramble under the rusty mesh of the drain that Leonard had noticed only a few minutes before.

"You stay on top and see where this thing ends," Noah ordered. "I'm going after that mutt."

He wrenched off the wire meshing and crawled into a dark wet tunnel.

Watson, paw deep in water, heard loud splashing noises behind him. He sped forward, making a hasty turn when the drainpipe suddenly swerved in another direction.

Behind him, head bent down and crawling as fast as he could, Noah failed to see the turn. *Thump.* The sound of his head hitting the drainpipe wall echoed along the length of the tunnel. Watson put on even more speed.

Ahead, some light filtered into the tunnel from an overhead grating and the hollow sounds of Watson's and Noah's chase caught Keith's ear. He quickly spotted the grating and bent over it. "Am I going the right way?" he called into it. "It's hard to tell."

Noah's hollow-sounding voice came back loudly.

"How do I know?" he shouted back angrily. "Keep going!"

Just then the tunnel sloped steeply downward. Watson skidded along for a short distance before the surface beneath his paws flattened out again. Noah Baxter came sliding and sloshing after him.

Outside, Keith reached the end of the long drain-pipe where it hung out over Town Lake below.

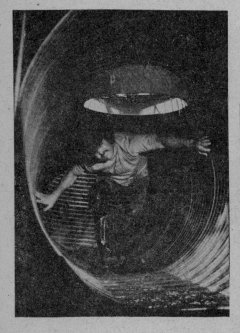

Carefully, he stretched out over it and took an up-side-down look into the pipe. "I see him!" he yelled. "Noah! You got him now!"

Watson could see that the situation was desperate. Behind him Noah Baxter was floundering onward. In the opening ahead of him, an upside-down face had suddenly appeared.

Deciding it was better to go on than go back, Wat-

son gathered himself for the big break to freedom, plunged ahead — straight out into space and made a daring dive into the lake below.

Flying through the air above him came Noah Baxter. And almost at the same moment, Keith Raynor made *his* dive for the Daumier jewels.

At the very last moment, Watson might have lost the race, except for one thing: Keith and Noah collided going into the water.

It was the chance that Watson needed. While the two men were still holding their heads, sputtering and treading water, Watson paddled briskly toward shore, the necklace still tightly held in his mouth.

To Keith Raynor and Noah Baxter, it was a terrible sight!

CHAPTER 6

Alfie Booth was still sound asleep, but the morning sunshine on Leonard's side of the room awakened him.

He blinked sleepily, yawned, and stretched — and suddenly his toes met damp, gritty sand.

He lifted the covers and peered down toward the foot of the bed. "Watson! What happened to you?"

Watson thumped his tail in a sleepy greeting, then immediately closed his eyes.

"What a mess!" Leonard said disgustedly, looking at the sandy sheet. "We've got to get it cleaned up before Mom sees it or you'll be sleeping outdoors from now on."

The little dog waded out of a tangle of sheets and

blankets—the slightly soiled Daumier necklace still dangling from his jaws.

Leonard's eyes widened. "Where'd you get this?" he asked as he took the necklace from Watson and rubbed it against his pajamas. The four rubies, set in gold, sparkled in the morning light.

"Wow!" he gasped.

"What's that?" Alfie spoke from his bed.

"It's mine," Leonard answered. "Watson gave it to me."

"That mutt been thieving again?" Alfie asked.

"He just found it," Leonard answered.

Alfie yawned. "Yeah — in some junkyard."

"You don't find gold and rubies in a junkyard," Leonard replied.

"Gold and rubies! Leonard, they're glass. *Anybody* would know that."

Leonard didn't bother answering. He swung the necklace in the light. Suddenly, and for the first time, he became interested in Alfie's movie.

"Dracula can wear it," he said generously.

Alfie sighed. "That's dumb. Dracula doesn't wear a necklace. He wears a ring."

"Why?"

"Because it's part of my story, that's why. That's what's left of Dracula after his body's gone."

"Ugh!" Leonard made a face.

Alfie got up and reached for the Dracula cape that

68

was flung over the back of a chair. He put it on and leaped up on his bed, waving his arms wildly over his head. "Sure. The stake is pounded in. Dracula turns into ashes. The wind spreads the ashes in the air. And all that's left is Dracula's ring. The *End*!"

"He could wear a necklace too," Leonard said stubbornly.

"A ring, Leonard, a ring — like the one we saw in the jewelry store!" Alfie jumped out of bed. "Hey! you might not be so far off after all. Maybe your necklace is worth something."

"What?" Leonard eyed Alfie suspiciously.

"Get dressed," Alfie ordered. "I've a great idea."

Noah Baxter was keeping a watchful eye on the Booth cottage. Sooner or later those kids would appear, and Noah planned to be around when they did. He slumped down in the Volkswagen and waited for Alfie, Leonard, and that villain, Watson.

Luck was with Noah. Mrs. Booth came to the door just as Leonard was slipping a rope leash over Watson's head. "Where are you going, boys?"

"Just to the jeweler's, Mom," Alfie said. "We'll be back soon."

"Jeweler's?" Mrs. Booth looked a little puzzled. "Well, all right, but be back in twenty minutes. Don't let Watson get into mischief."

That was all Noah needed to hear. He started the car and, looking straight ahead, drove past the boys.

Before heading for Bill Wasdahl's shop, he stopped at the lighthouse to pick up Keith.

Bill Wasdahl was polishing a silver teapot when the boys came into the shop. He looked up. "Get that dog out of here!" he exclaimed.

"Don't worry, Mr. Wasdahl, we've got him on a leash," Alfie said. "Anyway, we've come on business."

He turned to Leonard. "Show him the necklace, Leonard."

Leonard stepped forward and held it out.

Bill Wasdahl's eyes widened, and suddenly, he became very friendly. "I'll have to have a better look," he said smiling.

"It must be worth something," Alfie said. "About thirty dollars?"

"Afraid not," came the reply. "It's only costume jewelry."

"I bet it's worth as much as that Dracula ring," Alfie said.

Leonard pulled back. "Alfie! You said we would just find out if my necklace is worth anything."

Before Alfie could answer, Bill Wasdahl leaned across the counter. "You've been good kids...keeping that dog away and everything. Let me have the necklace. I'll trade it for the ring."

"Great! Leonard, give him the necklace."

Leonard pulled back again, and Alfie stepped over to him. "This is a good deal. Come on."

Bill Wasdahl smiled. "It's a lady's necklace. Not for a real boy like you."

"I like it," Leonard said stubbornly.

"Leonard!" Alfie pleaded. "*Trade*."

But Leonard turned and hurried to the shop door. Alfie rushed after him, and both boys nearly collided with Keith Raynor on his way into the shop.

"Hey, watch it! What's the matter?" Keith asked.

"Leonard won't trade that dumb necklace," Alfie said. "And we really need Dracula's ring instead."

Bill Wasdahl hurried around from in back of the counter. "I'll tell you what I'll do, Leonard. I'll give you two rings for it. One for each of you. Now that's downright generous."

Leonard's jaw set. "No!"

"What's so special about that necklace?" Keith asked.

"It's rubies and gold," Leonard said. "That's special."

Keith smiled. "Really? May I see it?"

Leonard unclasped his treasure and handed it over.

"It's just costume jewelry," Bill Wasdahl said.

Keith nodded. "Yes. And some of the stones are missing too. Can't be worth much."

"I don't care." Leonard reached out for the necklace.

Keith lifted it a little higher. "I could use it, though. I'm working on a collage now where these might fit in. A collage is —

"I know," Leonard said quickly. "We make them in school all the time. You can use shells and scraps of almost anything."

Keith looked at him. "You're right, of course. But Leonard, these fake rubies would help me a lot, and I'd pay you hard cash. How much are you willing to sell them for?"

Leonard grabbed the necklace dangling from Keith's fingers. "I'm not selling," he said firmly, stuffing it into his pocket.

There was a tense silence, then Alfie spoke. "Okay. Let's go home. I've got a movie to make."

Keith Raynor's thoughts raced. How could he get the necklace back? And what about Noah, who was standing guard across the street? What would he say if Keith came out of the jewelry shop without the Daumier necklace?

Suddenly Keith smiled. "Alfie, I'll have some free time tomorrow. Would you like to film inside the lighthouse?"

Alfie's eyes glowed. "In Dracula's Castle? Really?"

Keith nodded. "There's only one thing — no dog."

"Watson goes wherever I go," Leonard said.

Alfie ignored this. "You have a deal, Mr. Raynor," he grinned. "But Jean will have to come. Jean Wyndham. She's Dracula's victim."

Keith frowned and hesitated. "Well, all right. Okay." He patted Leonard's shoulder, looked past him at Bill Wasdahl, and grinned triumphantly.

Noah Baxter watched as Keith worked on the fake necklace that they planned to switch with the Daumier original. Keith had given up working in the lantern gallery. It was inconvenient and at night it was too conspicuous.

"Aren't you finished yet?" Noah grumbled. "We don't have forever you know."

Keith lifted a piece of red glass and set it into position. "Don't rush me," he said slowly. "This has to look right."

"Come on!" Noah exclaimed. "That kid isn't going to spot the difference when we switch them."

"He might," Keith replied.

Noah grunted, turned away, and picked up the box containing the dynamite. He started for the stairs.

"Where are you going with that?" Keith asked, looking up.

"Locking it up in the lantern gallery with the rest of the dynamite — and the fireworks you bought for your guests. You and your big ideas...telling those kids they could film their dumb picture here." Noah's voice trailed off as he circled up the iron stairs.

When he returned to the workroom he was carrying the empty box.

"What'd you unpack it for?" Keith asked.

"You do your work and I'll do mine," Noah replied. "Just get that necklace finished, Raynor."

Noah Baxter couldn't have done a nicer thing, Alfie felt, when they arrived for the filming next day. His toughest prop problem had been finding a coffin for Dracula — and the pine dynamite box was just about the right size for Alfie's leading man.

In fact, Leonard, lying in it with eyes closed, pearly fangs glinting, and a touch of catsup on his lips and chin, looked horrible enough even for Alfie.

"Mr. Baxter," Alfie said excitedly, "you stand here and hold the movie light so it shines down on Dracula. Wow! The necklace looks great! Jean, when you come up, you look revolted, but you bravely hammer in the stake right through Dracula's heart. Then, Dracula, you — "

Keith interrupted. "Alfie, isn't that too... er, realistic? It sounds dangerous to me."

Alfie shook his head. "Don't worry, Mr. Raynor. It's the effect I'm after. Actually, Jean hammers down the stake in the space between Dracula's ribs and his arm. But it will look great."

Alfie turned toward his cast. "Okay. Keep your eyes closed, Leonard, and remember to shriek when you feel the stake is driven in. Now, positions please. Action."

Jean, her hair piled high on her head, and wearing the evening gown she had worn at the Junior Prom, closed in on Dracula. She shuddered, put the stake in place, and lifted the hammer high.

Wham! Leonard shrieked loudly, and Alfie called out, "Great shot. You can get up now, Leonard."

Keith tilted the light away, and Leonard started to sit up. "I can't," he said anxiously. "Something must have happened to me!"

Alfie sighed and walked over to the pine box. "Leonard, nothing's happened to you. Your cloak is just nailed to your coffin — that's all." He tugged at the stake. It wouldn't budge.

"Here," Keith elbowed Alfie aside. "Let me try it."

He pretended to struggle with the stake as he felt in his pocket for the fake necklace in case a quick switch could be made.

But it was hopeless. Too many pairs of eyes were watching, and both men realized it. So Keith quickly jerked the stake free. "There you are, kid. Dracula can rise from his coffin again!"

"Okay," Alfie said briskly, as his brother was helped out of the pine box. "Next setup. On the stairs. Makeup!"

"*Next* setup!" Noah exclaimed. "I thought you'd just killed off Dracula."

"Oh, I can work that in anywhere," Alfie replied.

"What I need now is something with real atmosphere." He turned to Jean. "This time I'll film the action on the stairs, using your shadows on the walls. You'll run up the stairs, Jean. Leonard, you'll follow. Okay. Lights, please. Action."

Alfie's idea was good, but he hadn't counted on Dracula tripping on his long cape and stumbling forward. "Cut!" he called. "Now we'll start again. Leonard, watch that cape. Action!"

This time, Dracula made it safely up the stairs. Jean, a terrified expression on her face, thrust out her arm. Dracula hissed, took a step backward, and grabbed for the staircase railing. He missed.

"Leonard!" Jean screamed.

Noah Baxter sprang up the stairs. Before Leonard could fall, Noah caught him — and caught the Daumier necklace too.

"Thanks, Mr. Baxter," Leonard said. "It's this stupid cape. Alfie, do I have to wear it?"

"We have to have this scene," Alfie answered heartlessly.

"But in a safer location," Jean said, her voice firm.

"The shadows — " Alfie began to say. Then he had an idea. "What about trapped on the walkway that goes around the top of the lighthouse? That would be great. The only escape — hundreds of feet down the jagged rocks and the crashing waves!"

"You mean the walkaway around the lantern gal-

lery," Keith said. He glanced at Noah. "What do you think?"

Noah nodded. "Why not?"

Everybody but Noah Baxter started to climb up to the lantern gallery. He lingered behind to place the fake necklace on the iron steps where Leonard could find it later. But as he took it from his pocket, a "ruby" fell out, *plinked* on the iron steps and shattered on the floor below. Noah frowned, then he pocketed the fake necklace once again and went on up the stairs to join the others.

Out on the walkway, he and Keith exchanged glances. "I started to explain to our guests how the light and foghorn used to help the ships at sea," Keith said, "but Alfie wanted to get right on with his filming."

Alfie hardly glanced at Noah. He placed Jean's hands on the iron railing that circled the lantern gallery. "There, that's good. Now you lean back and look terrified. Are you ready, Leonard?"

Leonard stepped forward, adjusting the neck of his cape. "My necklace!" he gasped. "It's gone!"

Noah Baxter grinned and held up the fake. "Found it on the stairs, Leonard. Here you are."

But as Leonard reached out for it, Noah let the necklace slide from his fingers. It plummeted to the rocks below.

"Noah!" Keith Raynor cried out sharply.

Noah shrugged. "Sorry, kid!"

Leonard dashed into the lantern gallery and ran for the stairs. Alfie and Jean sped close behind him.

Keith glared at Noah. "That was a rotten thing to do."

Noah leaned his elbows on the railing and looked down at the rocks. "You said yourself that the kid might not be fooled. Besides, a so-called ruby fell out of it. Some work you do!"

Keith's hands clenched. Then he turned away and hurried after the boys and Jean.

He reached them none too soon. Almost at the very edge of the cliff, Leonard was wiggling out of Alfie's grasp. "But I can *see* it," he was saying desperately. "It's right down there on the rocks." He moved his foot and loose stones began sliding and clattering down the steep slope. Far below, surf smashed against the rocks and salt spray rose high in the air.

"Leonard, you can't go down there," Alfie cried, clutching his brother.

Keith caught Leonard's shoulders and pulled him back. "Leonard," he said gently, "you'll never reach it. Forget it. I think we've all had enough for a while. How about a break? Ice cream sound good?"

As the four walked back to the lighthouse, Leonard looked back at the cliff edge. And high above them, Noah Baxter watched them with a tight little grin.

"Tough luck, kid," he muttered cynically.

CHAPTER 7

Back again at the cottage, Alfie sat at the kitchen table designing titles for his film. Across from him, Leonard and Watson watched Jean add a few drops of steak sauce to the bowl of catsup she was mixing.

She set it down and tilted it toward Alfie. "Sir, the blood is ready," she said.

Alfie glanced at it. "Mmm. Say, Jean — which of these titles do you like best? *Horror of Dracula; Dracula, Prince of Darkness; Dracula Risen from the Grave;* or *Scars of Dracula*? All the really good titles have been taken."

Jean eyed Watson as he hopped up on a chair and sampled the contents of the bowl. He licked his chops in a pleased way. "How about *Taste the Blood of Dracula*," she suggested.

"It's been used," Alfie answered. "Leonard, we'd have the ideal title if you'd only traded that necklace for the ring when I told you to. I'd have called it *The Deadly Ring of Dracula*. Now I can't even call it *The Deadly Necklace of Dracula*."

Leonard didn't reply. He left the kitchen with Watson at his heels.

Five minutes later, Watson was riding in the bike carrier as Leonard, fishing rod over his shoulder, pedaled toward the lighthouse — and the cliff.

At the cliff's edge, Watson's enjoyment of the outing came to a sudden end.

"Stay," Leonard commanded.

Watson didn't mind "staying" at all. Nothing could have tempted him to go down over the edge of the cliff. It was Leonard's *not* staying that was ruining the afternoon. Watson woofed and whined anxiously as he watched Leonard lower himself over the craggy rocks.

Holding a fishing rod in one hand and grabbing at rocks with the other was no easy job. Leonard tried not to look all the way down to the dizzying foam that swirled around the base of the cliff.

Inch by inch, Leonard moved to a narrow foothold where he could press his back against the rock wall to steady himself. And there he made his first try with hook and line to catch the necklace on the rocks below.

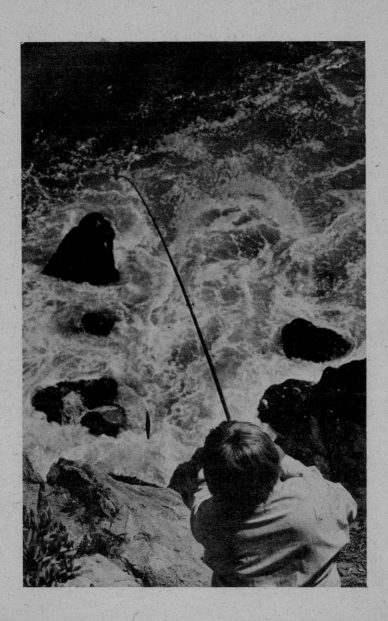

He lowered the line until the hook nibbled at the necklace. It didn't catch. Leonard reeled in a bit and tried again. This time he felt the hook grab. Excitedly he reeled in. Up, up, came the necklace, swaying gently. Then, to Leonard's dismay, the line caught fast in a crevice in the rocks.

There was only one thing to do — and Leonard did it. He began to edge his way down the steep face of the cliff. Small rocks loosened beneath his sneakers and he could see the sickening plunge they made to the sea below. Fear choked his throat. He knew he must keep his eye on the necklace and think of nothing else. One step at a time. Another, then another. And there was the necklace within reach! He worked the line free and then stuffed the necklace in his pocket.

It wasn't until he looked up the cliff that Leonard realized his terrible danger. Sliding and grabbing his way down had been bad, going back looked impossible.

With every reach and push of his sneakers, rocks loosened and clattered down and off into space. In one dreadful slip, Leonard felt himself dangling in air. Only his hands held. Desperately he kicked his legs, found another foothold, and the struggle to the top began again.

Watson was watching all this so intently that he never noticed the arrival of his old enemy, Bill Wasdahl. But Leonard did. Two shoes came into view just as he was making a grab for the grass edge at the cliff top. But as his fingers clutched at it, the soil began to break away. For one dreadful moment Leonard was sure he'd lost his chance of reaching the top.

"Watson!" he screamed.

Almost as he began to hurtle backward, one of the jeweler's shoes came at him.

"Grab, boy! Grab my ankle!" Bill Wasdahl shouted.

Seconds later, he was standing safe and sound and looking up at Bill Wasdahl.

"Are you all right?" the jeweler asked.

Too shaken to speak, Leonard nodded.

"What are you doing here?" Bill Wasdahl asked.

"Fishing," Leonard gasped.

"Fishing!" Bill Wasdahl looked at Leonard suspiciously.

Leonard nodded. "Yes, I was."

Bill Wasdahl frowned. "Come on. I'll take you home. I want to make sure your mother knows where I found you 'fishing.'"

"Oh — you needn't bother, Mr. Wasdahl," Leonard answered quickly. "I have my bike."

"No bother. We'll take that along too. Don't worry."

But Leonard Booth was very worried. "This will be worse than the cliff!" he thought miserably.

As soon as Bill Wasdahl left, Marsha Booth hugged Leonard close. "Leonard, you could have been *killed.*"

"I wasn't," Leonard replied uneasily, knowing the worst was to come.

"You could have been. And that settles it." She looked from Leonard to Alfie. "Boys, you're *both*

confined to the house for a week. And Jean, it's your job to see that they're *both* all right."

Jean flushed. "I know, Mrs. Booth."

"Mom!" Alfie said angrily. "Why should *I* be confined to the house? I didn't do anything."

"No, you didn't," his mother said. "And that's just it. You're Leonard's older brother. You should have been looking out for him too."

Like Jean, Alfie flushed. "I guess you're right, Mom."

Mrs. Booth left the room and Alfie threw himself into a chair and glared at Leonard. "And now how am I going to finish my picture?" he asked.

"I had to get the necklace," Leonard said stubbornly.

"You and that stupid necklace," Alfie snapped. "And you didn't even get it back."

"Yes I did," Leonard said. He pulled it from his pocket. Where there had been four "rubies," now there were only three — and they were not nearly as shiny and glowing as Leonard remembered. He walked away and picked up his magnifying glass.

Alfie thumped his heels on the floor. "We might as well send out the invitations to the opening," he said gloomily. "I'll get my prints back in a couple of days, and I'm not going to be able to add anymore scenes to this movie — I can see that. Did you finish the list, Jean?"

Jean nodded. "Here it is. Your mom, my father, and — "

Leonard walked in. "I knew it. There's something wrong with this necklace. The color's different and — "

Jean glanced up and away again. "Looks all right to me," she said. She turned back to Alfie. "I'm asking Keith Raynor and Noah Baxter — and Mr. Wasdahl too. How's that?"

"Great!" Alfie exclaimed. "Jean, this is going to be *big*."

Jean laughed. "I know. Red carpets, flowers, everything."

"Sure," Alfie said seriously. "I want it to be a regular Hollywood premiere."

Leonard could see that nobody was really interested in listening to him. "Come, Watson," he said.

Leonard's next try was his mother. Maybe she'd listen. "Mom, it's my necklace. Something's wrong. It's changed. I just *know* it's different."

Mrs. Booth turned away from her typewriter. "Sounds as though you have a real mystery on your hands."

Leonard nodded. "That's what I think."

"Have you any suspects?" his mother smiled. "In my books, the person most unlikely to commit a crime is the one who is the criminal. Has anybody shown an interest in the necklace?"

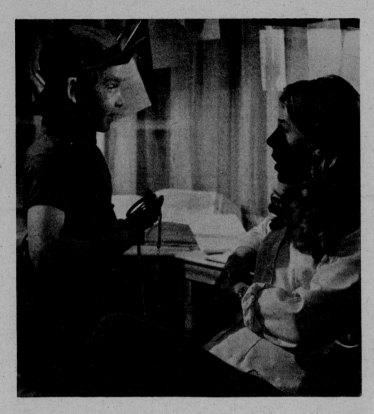

Long after Leonard had gone to bed he was thinking of the right answer to his mother's question. Scenes flashed into his mind. Noah had said it was nice. Keith said he could use it for a collage. Bill Wasdahl had offered him a trade. Jean liked it, and Alfie had wanted to use it for a trade. "In the morning, first thing, I'm going to make a list of suspects," he thought sleepily. "First thing."

Right after breakfast, Leonard started his questioning with Jean. "Sure I said your necklace was pretty, Leonard." She smiled. "But I'm a beads person myself. I'm going to need help with the cookies for the party. Are you going to be around?"

Leonard quietly crossed Jean's name off the list.

Alfie was next, but Leonard found it hard to believe Alfie was a real suspect. He drew a line through Alfie's name. "That leaves only Noah Baxter and Keith Raynor," Leonard said to himself. "But if they'd really wanted the necklace, they could have gone down the cliff themselves. I'd never have seen it again. I might as well give up. Without them I just don't have any suspects."

He put the list in his pocket. As he started out of the kitchen, a question popped into his mind. "What would Sherlock Holmes do right now?" And Leonard knew the answer. "He wouldn't give up," he said aloud.

"What did you say, Leonard?" Jean asked.

"Oh — nothing," Leonard replied.

CHAPTER 8

Sheriff Wyndham's car was already parked in the Booth's driveway when Noah Baxter and Keith Raynor arrived for Alfie's premiere.

"I don't like this," Noah grumbled. "Suppose the sheriff recognizes the necklace in the movie?"

Keith Raynor laughed. "That small-town hayseed? Forget it. Come on. Let's get this over with."

Both men managed to smile when Marsha Booth greeted them at the front door. Alfie's premiere seemed to be getting off to a great start. Everything was ready — from lighted candles on the refreshment table to eerie music on the phonograph.

Leonard, wearing the necklace, went from person to person with a plate loaded with cookies. "Hi, Mr. Baxter. Want a cookie?"

Noah Baxter's hand went out — and stopped. He stared at Leonard's necklace. "How — ?"

Keith Raynor hastily spoke. "I see you got your necklace back. That's great."

Leonard didn't blink. "I got it with my fishing line, but it's not mine."

Keith tried to smile. "Oh? Whose is it?"

"I don't know," Leonard answered. "But I'm going to find out."

Keith shrugged. "If you want my opinion, it's the same ordinary costume jewelry you had before. Unfortunately, I've finished the collage I was working on. I don't want it."

"Oh." Leonard's voice showed his disappointment. Mentally, he crossed Keith's name off the list of suspects.

He looked at Noah Baxter. "Have another cookie, Mr. Baxter. Do you think dreams mean anything?"

"What?" Noah reached for a cookie.

"I had a dream about you. I dreamed you took my necklace."

Noah suddenly uncrossed his legs. His foot hit the bottom of the loaded cookie plate and cookies rolled in all directions. He bent over to help pick them up. "Now look what you made me do," he said, trying to laugh. "You just had a dream, kid. I never wanted your necklace."

Leonard stared at him suspiciously. He turned

away, put down the cookie plate, took out his suspect list, and quickly circled Noah Baxter's name.

"Okay, everybody. Sit down. We're ready to start," Alfie called out. "Leonard, will you turn off the lights?"

Jean turned on the record player, and to the strains of chilling, stirring music, Alfie's masterpiece began.

Across the screen, the title loomed up — *Dracula and the Sheriff's Daughter*. Next came the credits — Directed, Produced, Written, Photographed, Edited, and Scored by Alfred Booth.

Everybody clapped and concentrated on the screen — everybody but Noah Baxter. He still had his mind on Leonard. "That kid's up to something," he thought uneasily. He glanced toward Leonard's chair.

It was empty.

On the cliff, the lighthouse loomed against the sky, pale as a tombstone beneath the moon and stars. From the rocks below came the boom of crashing surf.

Leonard propped his bike against a dark clump of bushes. Then, picking up Watson and the flashlight he had brought along, he started up the driveway.

Watson scampered on ahead and was already scratching at the door by the time Leonard reached it. Leonard turned the knob. Locked. "Maybe they've left a window open. Come on, Watson," Leonard said.

There was no window open, but he found a small window in the storage room that was unlocked. Leonard opened it easily. But before he could even turn on his flashlight, Watson vanished over the window sill.

"Watson! Wait!" Leonard cried. "Come back here!"

A faraway, cheerful bark came from the darkness. Leonard flashed his light and followed Watson into the lighthouse. The strong beam of the flashlight fell on the burned out wall safe but no Watson was in sight. Fearfully, Leonard moved on until a noise from above brought him to a sudden stop. It was Watson on the stairs outside the second floor workshop.

"Come on down here!" Leonard called. "We're supposed to be searching *together*."

Watson signaled with a departing wag of his tail and trotted on into the workroom. Leonard hesitated a moment, then hurried up the stairs. "You're supposed to be following me — not me following — " He broke off as his glance went to the worktable.

Twisted in a golden glitter was the Daumier necklace. "My necklace!" Leonard exclaimed. He hurried over to pick it up. Not a ruby was left!

While he was still staring at the remains of the once beautiful necklace, headlight beams flashed across the room and Leonard heard the roar of the Volks-wagen zooming up the drive.

Grabbing the necklace, he scooted to a window. The drop below was much too far. Frantically, he looked around. As footsteps sounded on the stairs, he swept Watson up in his arms and crawled under the worktable. He bumped against a heavy wooden box — the coffin box. Leonard shuddered and held Watson closer. "Don't bark," he begged.

Keith Raynor and Noah Baxter walked in. Leonard could see their shoes. Then his view widened as the two men crossed the room and went straight to a small steel box. Keith opened it and lifted out seven glowing rubies set in a brand new necklace.

"One thing I'm sure of," Keith said. "Nobody will recognize the Daumier jewels now."

"The Daumier jewels!" Leonard gasped to himself. "Of course! They were stolen from Mr. Flack!"

"Let's celebrate," Keith was saying. "A hundred thousand dollar necklace in the clear is worth a toast. I'll go down and get some drinks."

"The fence ought to be getting here any minute," Noah said.

Keith laughed. "Yeah. Bill isn't going to recognize the jewels now. I'll be back in a second."

Fence — that would be the man who was going to sell the stolen jewels for them. Leonard listened as Keith's footsteps on the staircase faded away.

Two shoes moved over by the table. "I know you're there, kid. I can see your mutt's tail. Come on out," a hard voice said.

There was a moment's absolute silence, then — WHAM! Leonard shoved hard on the pine box. It went hurtling out — straight into Noah Baxter's shins. In the same second Leonard and Watson shot out from the other side of the table. Leonard swerved to snatch the necklace from the steel box, then made a rush for the stairs.

"Keith!" Noah yelled. "Get him!"

But Keith, tray in hand, was no match for Leonard or Watson. They plowed past him and were out the front door before Keith realized what was happening.

"After them!" Noah shrieked, hobbling down the stairs as fast as he could. "They've got the necklace!"

In the darkness beyond the lighthouse entrance, Leonard crashed straight into a man heading for the doorway.

"Help! Help!" he cried out. "They're after me! They're jewel thieves!"

"Bill," Noah shouted. "Grab that kid. He's got the jewels!"

Bill! That was the name of the man Noah had called "the fence"! Too late Leonard realized he was begging the wrong person for help. He struggled in the iron grip of the man standing in the dark. "Let me *go*!" he cried — and looked up.

To his amazement, he saw Bill Wasdahl, the town jeweler. And his name hadn't even appeared on the suspects list that Leonard had left in the kitchen!

In the storage room of the lighthouse, the three jewel thieves clustered together. "You can't keep that kid locked up there in the lantern gallery," Bill Wasdahl said. "That's kidnapping. I didn't expect anything like this."

"Who's kidnapping?" Noah Baxter asked. "They'll find him by tomorrow, and by that time we'll be long gone. I'm not sticking around here to become a ward of the state. And you take my advice — get yourself out of the country too, while there's still time."

Bill's eyes widened. "You can count me out of this deal," he said. And, without adding another word, he brushed past Keith and Noah. The door banged behind him.

Seconds later, the headlights of his car picked out the figures of Alfie Booth and Jean Wyndham trudging up the driveway. He ducked his head and sped past them.

"Hi!"

Noah Baxter's hand froze on the handle of the Volkswagen door. He swung around. "Jean! Alfie! What are you doing here?"

"Leonard's missing," Jean said. "We think he's

around here somewhere. Mrs. Booth is out in her car looking for him, and my dad is searching too. We decided to come here."

"His bike's down there in the bushes," Alfie said. "We spotted it."

Keith stepped around from the other side of the car. "Well, let's take a look," he said. "Come on, Noah. We'll search the place from *bottom to top*."

Noah looked doubtful, but he followed the group into the lighthouse.

On the first floor they found the window open in the storage room. On the second floor, Jean discovered Leonard's flashlight where it had rolled out from under the worktable. Keith took it and frowned. "We'd better go up to the lantern gallery. That's the last place to look."

But at the top of the stairs, Alfie saw that the trapdoor was bolted. "He wouldn't be there, Mr. Raynor. It's locked from this side."

"Better look," Keith replied, unbolting the door.

"Yeah, better look," Noah Baxter growled.

And almost before Jean and Alfie knew it, they had joined Leonard and Watson in the dark lantern gallery — pushed in by Keith and Noah.

"Alfie! Jean!" Leonard gulped. "They're jewel thieves! My necklace — it was the Daumier jewels!"

The bolt on the trapdoor thudded into place. For a second there was dead silence in the round, glass room high above the crashing surf. Then Alfie yelled out, "We've got to stop them. We've *got* to!"

"How?" Jean asked hopelessly. "We can't even signal for help. Mr. Raynor took the flashlight."

Alfie bounded to the windows overlooking the driveway. "They haven't left yet," he said excitedly.

"What's the difference?" Jean said gloomily. "We're stuck here."

"Maybe not! I've got the matches I used to light the candles on the refreshment table," Alfie said.

Leonard shook his head. "You can't signal with matches, and there aren't any candles here."

But Alfie had other ideas. He struck a match and made his way to the old instrument panel. "The foghorn. It works from here somewhere. That'd bring help!"

"We should have let Mr. Raynor show us how things worked," Jean said. "He was going to when we were filming — "

Alfie interrupted. "I'll pull everything. *Something* ought to start!" He stared at the switches and dials. "Here goes!"

In seconds, the bellow of the foghorn came blasting in their ears, and the huge old lamp that once guided ships at sea began to glow dimly. Then its light quickly died down.

"No oil," Jean said desperately.

But in the dying light, Leonard spotted the sign on

one of the two wooden boxes Noah had carried up to the lantern gallery. "Fireworks!" he exclaimed.

"That solves our signal problem!" Alfie shouted. "Come on!"

Leonard frowned. "That's funny," he thought. "The 'fireworks' box downstairs had 'Dynamite' written on the side of it."

But this was no time for just *thinking*, and Leonard

rushed to help Alfie unload stacks of red-wrapped roman candles packed in a bed of straw.

Down in the doorway, as Keith and Noah headed for the Volkswagen, the sudden roar of the foghorn split the air. And almost before the first bellow died away, a roman candle came hissing downward, exploding in a burst of red and green stars.

"Fireworks! Those blasted kids found the fireworks!" Keith exclaimed.

"You and your fireworks!" Noah shouted angrily. "Let's get out of here!"

They hurriedly tossed their luggage into the Volkswagen. But before they could climb in themselves, three more roman candles came hurtling down almost on top of them. In a fiery shower of gold, silver, red, blue, and green stars, the two men dashed for cover.

CHAPTER 9

In the brilliant light of the exploding fireworks, Alfie had a clear view of Keith and Noah scurrying away from the Volkswagen.

"Keep 'em coming, Leonard," he shouted back from his lookout on the walkway. "We've got 'em on the run!"

Inside the lantern gallery, Leonard and Jean worked at top speed to keep Alfie in fireworks ammunition. Leonard was in charge of lighting the fuses and handing the candles on to Jean. She acted as the supply line and dashed from Leonard to Alfie with each sputtering explosive.

"Here you are, Alfie," she panted. "Fire away!"

She waited a second on the walkway to watch the spectacular star-burst that followed Alfie's well-aimed pitch, then rushed back inside. "Leonard!" she screamed. "*Watch out!*"

Leonard was staring in horror at the roman candle in his hand. The lighted fuse was burning much too fast and its glowing tip snaked along at lightning speed toward the explosive charge.

"Throw it!" Jean screamed.

As she and Leonard ran for cover, the released candle exploded in a hissing blast of light. Smoke filled the small room and sparks fell like fiery raindrops.

On the walkway, Alfie whirled around. "Jean! Leonard! You okay?" he shouted.

"The room's on fire," Jean shouted back.

Alfie took a deep breath and dove inside. His eyes smarted in the smoke-filled air, which was now turning an ugly dull pink. Jean was swatting at the flames with her jacket, and Leonard was hopping up and down like a jack-in-the-box, stamping out curls of flame that glowed on the floor.

Then, in one stinging, tear-filled glance, Alfie saw the most dreadful sight of all — dark letters showing clearly in the light of the flames that flared and crept along the sides of a wooden box: DYNAMITE. Then he remembered Keith's words: "Dynamite? Oh, you must mean my *fireworks*."

Alfie tore off his T-shirt and began batting at the flames. "Let's get this fire out!" he shouted, "or there's going to be plenty more fireworks — *plenty*."

Noah Baxter lifted his face from the sand. He saw the pinkish glow in the lantern gallery. "Keith!" he exclaimed. "Get up! We've got to get out of here."

Keith Raynor looked up. "It's on fire!" he exclaimed, horrified. "Noah — the dynamite! We've got to get those kids out of there!" He sprang to his feet and ran toward the lighthouse.

Noah raced behind him. He leaped into the Volkswagen. "Come on!" he shouted. "This is our one chance!"

Keith shouted back. "You put the dynamite up there. Those kids could be killed!"

"I'm not staying," Noah yelled back, starting the engine.

"I'm no murderer," Keith yelled. "I've got to let those kids out."

"Be the hero," Noah screamed after Keith. "I'm leaving." He swung the Volkswagen down the drive.

Too late! Sheriff Wyndham's patrol car, siren sounding and red warning light revolving, swung off the road into the drive.

Noah stopped and got out of the little car, hands raised over his head.

Sheriff Wyndham climbed out of the patrol car and ran up the driveway. "What's the idea?" he said angrily. "You know fireworks are illegal in this county."

Noah Baxter's jaw dropped. He was so sure he was

about to be arrested that now he couldn't believe his
ears. "I just — "

There was a sudden hissing, swishing sound above
them. Both Noah and the Sheriff rushed out of range
of the exploding stars and almost ran into the headlights of Marsha Booth's car, which came to a
screeching stop.

Above them, the flames suddenly shot out from the

lantern gallery. "What's going on?" Marsha Booth asked anxiously.

"You can't pin this on me," Noah Baxter said nervously. "I'm no killer."

Sheriff Wyndham and Marsha Booth stared at him in amazement. "Can't pin *what* on you?" the Sheriff asked. "What are you talking about?"

Noah squirmed. "The kids. Keith. They're up there."

"No!" Marsha Booth cried. She started forward. But as the Sheriff pulled her back, Keith, Jean, Alfie, Leonard, and Watson, came racing out of the lighthouse.

"*Run!*" Keith screamed. "*Run!* The dynamite! It's about to go!"

Like rabbits, seven people and one small dog bounded across the drive and down the road. As they flung themselves to the ground, there was an earth-shattering BOOM.

In one glorious burst of fireworks and one terrible blast of dynamite, the old lantern gallery blew sky-high!

When the last thudding blast died away, Watson scrambled up from the huddled group, shook off a small cloud of sand, and sneezed briefly. Ready for more action, he trotted off as the others were just getting to their feet.

"Alfie — Leonard! You could have been killed!"

Marsha Booth brushed the tears off her cheeks and hugged her sons.

In the moonlight, Sheriff Wyndham looked from the tattered, smoke-smudged boys and his own smudge-streaked daughter, to Keith and Noah. "Will someone kindly tell me what's going on around here?" he asked.

Leonard pointed to Keith and Noah. "They've got my necklace."

"Your *necklace*? *What* necklace?

"They're jewel thieves, Dad," Jean Wyndham said hotly. "Arrest them!"

"*Jewel thieves!*" Keith Raynor exclaimed. "Nonsense! I never heard anything so silly in — "

His words ended as Watson, who had been tearing at a knapsack on the front seat of Noah's car, skidded to a halt in front of Leonard.

"Watson!" Leonard cried. He bent down and took the necklace from Watson's jaws. "*This* isn't nonsense, Sheriff Wyndham. It's the Daumier jewels. And they're worth one hundred thousand dollars — Mr. Raynor and Mr. Baxter said so. They stole it, and Mr. Wasdahl is their *fence*."

Sheriff Wyndham's jaw dropped. "Bill Wasdahl! A crook!" The Sheriff's hand went to his gun holster and Keith and Noah backed up. "Okay, you two. We'll clear this up back in town. Get going."

CHAPTER 10

Sheriff Wyndham and Jean were helping Alfie and Marsha Booth lash the bicycles onto the back of the Booths' car.

"I'll never forget this summer," the sheriff said. "Bill Wasdahl mixed up with jewel thieves." He shook his head. "You folks coming back next summer?"

"We haven't missed a summer yet," Mrs. Booth replied gaily. She stowed her typewriter into one last space. "Alfie — where's Leonard? We're all set to go."

"I was going to ask the same thing," the sheriff said. "I've a little something here for him."

Alfie looked up interestedly. "What?"

Just then Leonard came around the corner of the cottage. He was walking very slowly and looking down at his sneakers.

"I can't find Watson anywhere," he said sadly.

"Oh, he'll show up," Sheriff Wyndham smiled. "Look, Leonard. I want you to have this." He held out a real deputy sheriff's badge and bent down to pin it on Leonard's shirt. "There now. It's official. You're my Special Deputy Sheriff. I couldn't have cracked this case without you."

Leonard's face brightened, but only for a second. Once again he looked down at his sneakers. "Thanks, but half of it belongs to Watson."

Alfie stared at his brother as though he were seeing Leonard for the first time. "*Half* the credit!" he thought. And suddenly he could see the credits at the beginning of his film — "Written by, produced by, photographed by, *everything* by Alfred Booth." "All the time I was laughing at him, he was sticking to being a detective and *he*'s the one who really cracked the case. He hasn't said once, 'I told you so.' And now here he is saying he should get only *half* the credit!"

Alfie cleared his throat. "Leonard — no wonder I call you 'dumb' sometimes! Can't you remember? *You're* Sherlock Holmes. And I bet Mr. Flack will be wanting to talk with you. Boy! Getting his jewels back and everything! That was something!"

Leonard still looked miserable. He shook his head.

"We'll have to go now, Leonard," his mother said gently. "We can't wait any longer for Watson." She turned to Sheriff Wyndham. "He's been gone since we started packing last night. I guess he is the town dog. We can't expect him to leave just because we have to go."

"Don't worry, Leonard," Jean said kindly. "I'll take good care of him while you're gone, and he'll be right here waiting for you next summer."

Marsha Booth got into the car. "Jump in, boys. Time to say good-bye."

Alfie climbed in and, slowly, Leonard followed. Marsha Booth switched on the motor. "Bye!" she called.

"See you next summer," Alfie grinned.

Leonard only lifted his hand in a sad wave. "But Watson's my partner," he said in a whispery voice.

"Bye!" the Wyndhams called after them. They watched the car move slowly down the street.

"Hey, Dad! Look!" Jean cried out.

Sheriff Wyndham tilted back his hat. "Well, I'll be darned! Looks like we're losing the town dog after all."

Watson, at top speed and barking his finest, raced after the Booths.

"Maybe they won't see him," Jean said anxiously.

"See him! They'll hear him," the sheriff laughed. "Don't worry!"

The two watched the Booth car slow to a stop. Leonard jumped out and swept up Watson in his arms. Then all three Booths turned to look back up the street. Three hands waved a happy, final farewell and there was a cheerful good-bye bark from Watson.

The Wyndhams waved back. "There goes Trouble," the sheriff grinned.

"There goes Watson, you mean, Dad. After all — "

"After all, what?" her father asked.

"After all," Jean said softly, "who ever heard of a Watson deserting a Sherlock Holmes? Especially the one who solved the mystery in Dracula's Castle?"